THIS LITTLE PIGGY

AN OWNER'S MANUAL

by Cyndi Marko

PIX™

ALADDIN PIX

New York   London   Toronto   Sydney   New Delhi

ALADDIN PIX

Simon & Schuster Children's Publishing Division
1230 Avenue of the Americas, New York, New York 10020
First Aladdin PIX hardcover edition June 2017
Copyright © 2017 by Cyndi Marko
All rights reserved, including the right of reproduction in whole or in part in any form.
ALADDIN and related logo are registered trademarks of Simon & Schuster, Inc.
ALADDIN PIX and colophon are trademarks of Simon & Schuster, Inc.
For information about special discounts for bulk purchases, please contact
Simon & Schuster Special Sales at 1-866-506-1949 or business@simonandschuster.com.
The Simon & Schuster Speakers Bureau can bring authors to your live event.
For more information or to book an event contact the Simon & Schuster Speakers Bureau
at 1-866-248-3049 or visit our website at www.simonspeakers.com.
Book designed by Laura Lyn DiSiena
The illustrations for this book were rendered in colored pencil, watercolor, and ink.
The text of this book was set in MetallophileSP8.
Manufactured in China 0317 SCP
2 4 6 8 10 9 7 5 3 1
Library of Congress Control Number 2016959832
ISBN 978-1-4814-6826-8 (hc)
ISBN 978-1-4814-6827-5 (eBook)

For Mom, who grounded me for not liking her garden. And for Dad, who didn't let me have a puppy. You big meanies. (But I 🖤 you.)

And ginormous thanks to my editor, Karen Nagel; my designer, Laura Lyn DiSiena; and my agent, Adriann Ranta, for their many contributions and their support in making Snowflake sparkle.

CHAPTER ONE

Have you always wanted a pet
with all your heart?

Cute ball of fur.

Slow and slimy.

Comes with a house.

Giddyup!

It seems like everyone you know has a pet.
Your friend Bowie's Saint Bernard rescues
mountain climbers.

Just last
week I saved
a family of
porcupines.

Squawk!
Uno, dos,
tres . . .

Your cousin Maya
has a parrot that
counts to ten.
In *Spanish*.

And your neighbor Mr. Bumble's cool chameleon changes color from pink to turquoise.

But I bet *you've* always wanted . . .

A PIG!
Pigs are AWESOME. They have:

a twitchy,
itchy snout,

flippy,
flappy ears,
and

Of course, your brother might
have other ideas. . . .

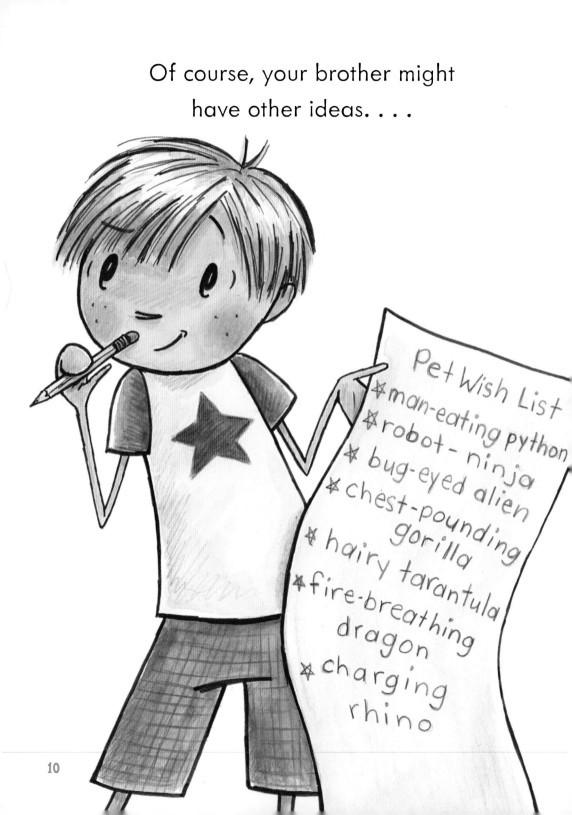

Pet Wish List
*man-eating python
*robot- ninja
* bug-eyed alien
* chest-pounding
gorilla
* hairy tarantula
*fire-breathing
dragon
* charging
rhino

You have to admit, a gorilla would be sort of neat. . . .

Yahoo! No more riding the bus to school!

P.U.

But on second thought, you sure wouldn't want to clean up after him.

Your brother might not care that pigs are louder than motorcycles,

have
forty-four teeth
(say "cheese"!),

and live on every continent except Antarctica,

Brrr—nobody here but us penguins.

oink oink oink

or that baby pigs
are called piglets.
Coochie, coochie, coo.

I know you can win him over!
Tell him that pigs . . .

love mud!

CHAPTER TWO

Getting your brother on board the
piggy train was the easy part.

Now you have to convince
your mother that there is no better
pet in the ENTIRE universe than a pig.
There is just one small problem:

your mother's favorite pets are from the *garden*.

You are right that garden plants are not pets. But try telling your mother that.

Obviously, you have your work cut out for you.
You'll need to hatch a scheme.

Remember when you wanted to eat ice cream for dinner?

Or wear your pajamas to school?

And how you had to fool (I mean, convince) your mom that those were great ideas? And she fell for it (I mean, agreed)?

To get your scheme started, make a checklist. Lists are great for staying organized. And by the look of this pigsty, you need help in that department

First pick a pig.
Try to pick one with *potential*.

project
pet pig
☐pick a
pig
☐give
pig
a bath

Amazingly, there's one—stuck in the mud.
He's your Snowflake.

CHAPTER THREE

Now that you've picked your pig,
let's move on.
Your pig is *terrifically* dirty, and
your mother only likes dirt in the garden.
Time for a bath! You'll need:

□ washtub

□ Soap
(extra sudsy)

□ water
(H$_2$O)

Once the washtub is filled to the brim,
the bath is ready for your pig.

No way.

Umm . . . where *is* your pig?

But you really don't want a pet rock.

(And sometimes you're not sure

you really want a brother. . . .)

Back to bathing.
Refill the tub with
warm soapy water.

Scrub your pig all over. Mom will love a clean
pig as much as she does a red pepper.

Scrub,
scrub, scrub,
one pig in
a tub.

Next, dry your pig with a soft towel.

That's one of your mother's fancy
guest towels—I'm sure she won't mind.

There. Your pig is clean as a whistle!

But *you* might need a bath.

CHAPTER FOUR

After his bath, your pig will be *super* hungry.
As everyone knows, a hungry pig is
a cranky, misbehaving pig.
Your mother will *never* approve,
so it's CHOW TIME!

Feed your pig

- □ bucket
- □ trough
- □ pig food

You'll need a slop bucket.

And a trough.

And look! Lucky you! There's Mom's garden,
with lots of yummy food for pigs.

Take juicy strawberries,

corn on the cob,

leafy spinach,

and ripe red tomatoes.

Mix it all together.

Lay out Mom's checkered tablecloth.

Dump the mixture in the trough.

Lunch is served.

Hmm, it seems as though something else has tickled your pig's nose . . .

Well, it's back to the second item on your list:
You have to bathe your pig all over again.

CHAPTER FIVE

Now that you've:

 picked your pig,

 cleaned your pig,

 fed your pig,

 and cleaned your pig again,

it's time to move on to the fun part:

TRICKS!

When you were younger, you might
have learned to:

juggle,

burp the
alphabet,

rub your stomach and
pat your head at the
same time,

or even do the
moonwalk.

Your mom was *so* proud.
I'm positive if your pig learns even a few tricks,
your mom will have to say yes!

Ask Snowflake
to juggle,

burp the
alphabet,

rub his stomach
and pat his head
at the same time,

or do the
moonwalk.

Well, at least there's one trick Snowflake
has learned. . . .

Oink.

CHAPTER SIX

It may appear that your scheme isn't exactly working.

Maybe you should take Snowflake to the county fair. He's blue-ribbon material!

Your mom can't say no to a prizewinning pig! (Remember, her petunias won the first-place prize.)

Golden Trowel Award

Snowflake is sure to be a front-runner
in the pie-eating contest.

49

Brother: - - - -
Sister: - - - - -
Snowflake: ♥

BUMPER CARS

TO EVEN MORE STUFF!

FACE PAINTING

CAROUSEL

PIE-EATING CONTEST

HAYRIDE

PETTING ZOO

COUNTY FAIR

However, I see you've clearly forgotten why you're there. Uh, remember your PIG?

SNOWFLAKE!

Don't go anywhere!

Oh, give me a home where the buffalo roam, and the deer and the piggies all play . . .

Once the Ferris wheel stops, you and your brother jump out and fetch your pig.

So maybe Snowflake is never clean, eats from the garbage, and can't do tricks.

But he's *your* pig.
Now is as good a time as any to head home . . .

to introduce Snowflake to your mother.

Oh, boy. I'm afraid your mother doesn't look very happy, does she?

But suddenly Snowflake takes off into the garden! Get out of here, you pesky crows!

Did I mention pigs make terrific scarecrows?

Did you hear that, you little schemers?
Mom said yes! Snowflake is all yours.

YAHOO!
How are you going to celebrate?

Cyndi Marko didn't have a pet pig when she was a kid. She did, however, scheme really hard for a puppy. She asked her dad for a puppy about a hundred times a day. In a row. Until he couldn't take it. And his eye began to twitch. She left drawings of puppies taped to his office door, on his chair, and in the bathroom. She begged, pleaded, made promises she totally didn't intend to keep, and even threw a tantrum or two. She never got a puppy, but he did, eventually, let her have a kitten. Hooray!

She thinks a pet pig would be pretty cool too, though.

Cyndi lives in Canada with her family and her two dogs. They chew everything. (Not the dogs; they're well behaved.)